STAR WARS
THE RISE OF SKYWALKER

Cover illustrated by Caleb Meurer
Interior illustrated by Alan Batson

 A GOLDEN BOOK • NEW YORK

rhcbooks.com

ISBN 978-0-7364-4076-9 (trade) — ISBN 978-0-7364-4077-6 (ebook)

Printed in the United States of America

10 9 8 7 6 5 4 3 2

A long time ago in a galaxy far, far away. . . .

The **Jedi**, Rey, trained in the ways of the **Force** with the help of her droid friend BB-8 and General Leia Organa, the leader of the **Resistance**.

The evil **First Order**—led by Leia's son, Kylo Ren, who had fallen to the dark side—was growing in power. But the Resistance refused to give up in their fight to free the galaxy.

Meanwhile, Kylo Ren used a Sith wayfinder to travel to a hidden planet called Exegol, where he discovered the evil **Emperor Palpatine**! Many years before, Leia and a group of Rebels had defeated the Emperor. But somehow the **Sith Lord** had returned.

The Emperor promised to give Kylo Ren an enormous fleet and all the **power** he needed to rule over the galaxy. But first, Kylo had to defeat Rey! Kylo assembled his elite band of warriors, the **Knights of Ren**, and had his old mask reforged. He was ready for anything!

Rey and her friends Finn, Poe, Chewbacca, C-3PO, and BB-8 blasted off in the *Millennium Falcon* to find a second wayfinder that could lead them to Exegol, so they could stop the Emperor.

Their search began on the desert planet Pasaana, where they met the Rebel hero **Lando Calrissian!**

Lando told them they might be able to find a clue in an old relic hunter's abandoned ship in the desert. Before the heroes could thank him, though, the First Order arrived! As **jet troopers** blasted from above, Rey and the others made a daring escape in speeders.

Rey and her friends ended up in sinking sands that pulled them down into a dark tunnel. There they discovered the old relic hunter's speeder, and a **dagger** with the location of a wayfinder carved into it in Sith markings.

C-3PO could read the message, but his programming wouldn't let him say it out loud.

Suddenly, the heroes ran into a **giant, scary** snake creature! Rey saw that the creature was hurt and used the Force to heal it.

The friends managed to escape from the tunnel, only to be spotted by Kylo and the Knights of Ren! Rey used her lightsaber to take down Kylo's TIE fighter, then used the Force to pull a First Order transport back to the ground. Kylo pulled at the transport through the Force, too.

Suddenly, **lightning** launched from Rey's hands, and the transport exploded! Rey was terrified by her own power.

BOOM!

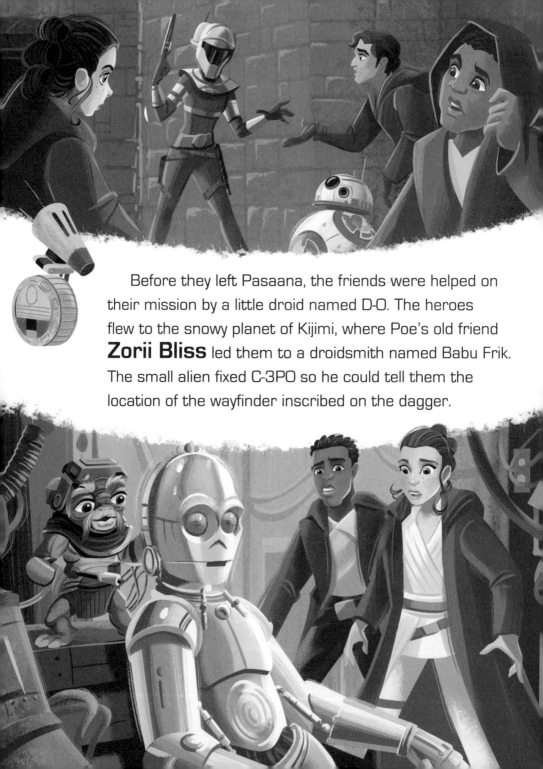

Before they left Pasaana, the friends were helped on their mission by a little droid named D-O. The heroes flew to the snowy planet of Kijimi, where Poe's old friend **Zorii Bliss** led them to a droidsmith named Babu Frik. The small alien fixed C-3PO so he could tell them the location of the wayfinder inscribed on the dagger.

The wayfinder was hidden on the ocean moon Kef Bir, in the wreckage of the Emperor's old Death Star—a superweapon that had been destroyed by the Rebels long before.

There, Rey and the others met **Jannah**, who had once been a stormtrooper, just like Finn. She warned them that the ocean was too dangerous to cross to get to the wreckage.

Rey knew they didn't have any time to lose, though, so she snuck off and sailed across the dangerous waves herself.

Rey soon found the wayfinder in the Death
Star wreckage, but Kylo Ren was waiting for her.
He tempted her to join the **dark side**.

He told Rey the evil Emperor
was her grandfather!
"No!" Rey cried.
She ignited her lightsaber
and **battled** Kylo as the ocean
waves crashed around them.

From across the galaxy, Leia used all of her strength to call out to her son through the Force, using the name she had given him—**Ben**.

As Leia became one with the Force, Kylo was distracted and Rey knocked him to the ground.

Leia was gone. And Rey had hurt her son. Quickly, Rey **healed Kylo** using the Force, then fled in his ship. She felt alone and scared. Had Kylo been right? Would she turn to the dark side?

Meanwhile, Kylo was visited by the memory of his father, **Han Solo**. Han reminded his son that it wasn't too late to do the right thing.

The young man threw his red lightsaber into the ocean. Kylo Ren was gone forever. He was finally Ben again.

Rey flew to the distant planet Ahch-To, set fire to Kylo's ship, and tossed her lightsaber into the flames. She was determined to hide on the island forever.

Suddenly, Jedi Master **Luke Skywalker** appeared through the Force, holding her lightsaber.

Luke was Leia's brother and Rey's former teacher.

"Confronting fear is the destiny of a Jedi," Luke said, presenting her with a second lightsaber—Leia's.

Luke's words made Rey realize that she had to face the Emperor. She grabbed Kylo's wayfinder from the burning TIE, but the ship was destroyed. How could she leave Ahch-To? Suddenly, Luke used the Force to raise his old **X-wing fighter** from the bottom of the ocean. Rey had everything she needed to save the galaxy!

Using the wayfinder, Rey flew to Exegol. She shared the coordinates with the Resistance so they could attack the Emperor's **massive** fleet of Sith Star Destroyers.

Finn and Jannah, riding creatures called orbaks, attacked the main ship's navigational tower that was directing the Sith fleet.

The heroes fought bravely, but they were outnumbered and were almost defeated.

Suddenly, ships from across the galaxy arrived.
Lando had convinced friends and allies to join the
fight! "The whole galaxy's here!" Poe cheered.

As the battle raged above, Rey confronted the evil Emperor, her grandfather. He urged her to join the dark side, but Rey would not give in to fear and hate. She was a Jedi, and she was **not alone**. Ben had arrived to help her! Rey sent Luke's lightsaber to him through the Force so Ben could defeat the Knights of Ren.

Together, Ben and Rey stood against the Emperor. But that was exactly what the Sith Lord wanted!

"The power of two restores the one true Emperor!" he hissed as he **drained** Rey and Ben of their life force and flashed deadly lightning from his hands!

The Emperor was strong! But Rey would not give up. She called upon all of the **Jedi of the past** for help through the Force. Then she deflected the Emperor's lightning back into the Sith Lord with Luke's and Leia's lightsabers, defeating him once and for all.

Rey had used all of her strength to defeat the Emperor, so Ben passed the last of his life force to her, saving her as she had saved him back on the Death Star. Finally at **peace**, Ben became one with the Force.

With the Emperor and his terrifying fleet destroyed, the galaxy was free once more! Rey traveled to Tatooine to **honor** her Jedi teachers Luke and Leia. They had given her all the strength and guidance she needed. Rey knew that no matter what the future held, she wouldn't face it alone.